Billy Bender
and
The Red Hot Ants

A tale from the "Outer Worlds Collection"

ARTICA BURR

Copyright © 2023 by Artica Burr.
Final Cover Design by John Michael Lozano
Back Cover Photo by Artica Burr

ISBN 979-8-89121-755-3 (softcover)
ISBN 979-8-89121-756-0 (hardcover)
ISBN 979-8-89121-757-7 (ebook)
Library of Congress Control Number: 2023913676

This book is a work of fiction. Names, characters, places, and incidents are the product of the author's imagination or are used fictitiously. Any resemblance to actual locales, events, or persons, living or dead, is purely coincidental.

Printed in the United States of America.

Artica Burr Publications
5040 Kraus Road
Clarence, NY 14031

Introduction

Through the Author's Windshield:

The characters in this book burst out of my file cabinet of potential characters. They insisted they were ready for adventure. I agreed that they were.

Although my subject matter varies concerning the fiction I write, my characters are always questing for a shred of the truth. Only some of the books I write are directed toward younger readers. But certainly, the concept of questing for the truth is best initiated before full-fledged adulthood when the grey areas of truth seep in. I have concluded that as one matures, the whole truth cannot be easily found because of the comfort found in self-deception.

I do not spin cotton candy plots, but my books lack the need for extreme graphic violence and unbridled horror. Most people can get more than their fill of that sort of thing on television or reading the world news.

.

Contents

Doom and Gloom for Breakfast

Chapter 1

Billy hunched over his cereal bowl. He tugged his baseball cap down so low it almost blocked his vision. The prospect of another day at school lay bleakly before him. He pressed his spoon into the bowl and watched the cereal circles struggle, pop up, and float on top of the milk like dozens of life preservers. They collided against one another as though they were begging to be eaten, but Billy had no appetite this morning. He stirred the cereal and watched the circles surface over and over; and then quietly sighed. Billy glanced over at his mother. When he was sure she was not looking, he reached into the box and slipped ten or so pieces of dry cereal into his pants pocket.

"Are you playing street hockey after school, Honey?" His mom, Maggie, asked while she busied herself grating cheese for her scrambled eggs.

"No chance," Billy grumbled. "Since Mark hit his head on the dumpster, the maintenance guy says we can't play hockey there anymore. I'm not sure there's anything a kid is allowed to do around here."

Billy sidled up to the counter and slipped a little chunk of cheese in his pocket as soon as his mother glanced away. "You know I hate living in an apartment. We used to have our own driveway. Remember? All they have here are rules, rules, and more rules. Living here actually stinks, Mom. Seriously, this place is the absolute pits."

Maggie felt her stomach tighten. The last year of their lives had been the aftermath of an unsettled, nightmarish situation. It depressed her too, but in front of Billy, she disguised her exasperation. "You know Billy, we both were used to living a different lifestyle. It'll take some time and effort on my part, but things will get back closer to how we used to live. I'm working hard at it, Billy, but right now, we have to start over. It's just you and me now, Honey. We will get there, I promise."

"Sure, it'll only take forever," Billy replied as he rummaged in his backpack.

"It was a terrible shame that Mark hurt his head. Who would think that he would ever back up into that metal dumpster and need to have eight stitches?" Maggie said while she stirred the eggs.

"I saw some kids playing hockey in the back parking lot over near the Catholic school. Bob's mom suggested you guys check it out after school. I'm sorry, Honey, but we just have to get through all this. Things will get better, I promise."

Billy quickly headed for the door. "Sorry doesn't change anything, and promises don't work for me anymore."

"Honey, wait. Don't forget your lunch." Billy's mom held out a brown bag and a bottle of iced tea.

"I'd rather buy my lunch today, thanks, and I owe for yesterday. When I opened my bag at lunchtime, there was an ant on my sandwich." Billy jammed the iced tea into his backpack and slid the money into his pocket.

"Well, I didn't try to pack it in there. Ants are simply showing up where you don't expect them. Everybody at the complex is complaining and waiting for the management to send in an exterminator. All we get is an answering machine. We all leave messages over and over."

"It's not going to happen. You picked this place, and living here is like living in a dump." Billy spun his hat around backward.

"Billy, please give things a chance. You complain about not making new friends, but with a better attitude, it might come easier. Smile once in a while and try to have a better day."

"Whatever. Like I really care." With all the finality that his twelve-year-old attitude could muster, Billy slammed the door.

"No pets, huh?" He mumbled once he was outside. "Well, some rules are made to be broken, and I'm keeping Mouse no matter what anybody says." He slipped a couple of cereal pieces into his shirt pocket, and the brown mouse began to munch on one of them while he peered up gratefully at Billy.

When the door closed, Maggie was left speaking to the four walls around her while she scooped her eggs onto a plate. "Billy, I sure wish I could find a way to help you lighten up and let me help you pull it together. You have to move on with your life. You're not alone in all of this. I'm still here for you." She spotted an ant in the mix, scraped the eggs into the sink, and listened to the dull grind of the garbage disposal.

It was a pleasant apartment if you liked apartment living. Selling the house was a forced issue she had to contend with because it was part of the divorce agreement. After living for years in a home of her own, Maggie no longer found apartment living appealing. She had to agree with Billy that there were more rules to abide by than freedom to enjoy living here. Maggie had promised herself that it was not a permanent solution for the two of them. The sooner she could afford to buy a house, the better both of them would feel, but the horizon on that goal was still more than a year away.

The rent she was paying wasn't cheap and certainly not worth this amount of aggravation. She would have to call once again and leave a message asking them exactly what date the pest control would come to take care of things. The ant traps she'd been using failed to phase these ants. Everybody in the apartment complex was seeing red over the situation and suffering from the recent invasion of ants.

It was getting hard for Maggie to tell which problem was growing faster; Billy's poor attitude or the number of ants in their apartment. She was ready to talk to the other tenants in the building to see if they wanted to hire an exterminator, and then all of them could perhaps deduct it from the rent. They should at least threaten the management before they threw caution to the wind and tried to pay and then deduct it.

Over Morning Coffee

Chapter 2

There was a quiet, familiar knock at the door, and Matt popped in for a few minutes after his night shift at the firehouse. Ever since he'd begun dating Maggie, he'd made it a point to stop to see her in the morning. He finished up work just before she had to leave for work.

Morning coffee together gave him the opportunity to gently reinforce the concept to Maggie that she actually did not have to face things all alone if she chose not to. If she needed help with anything, he was available so she could ask. In his own quiet way, he always found something to offer to do for her or suggested a place where they could all go together as a family. He could feel Maggie still needed some time after her divorce, and Matt was willing to respect that, but he enjoyed every moment he shared with her and with Billy.

"You look rested. Quiet night?" Maggie asked as she poured him a coffee.

"Yep, a rarity. All night long, it turned out that all was well. I got to catch a couple of winks of sleep in." Matt smiled.

Maggie looked forward to Matt's stopping by. He was always so positive, and his winning smile helped launch her day. The brief morning visits renewed her determination and belief that there was a light at the end of the tunnel that she and Billy were working their way through.

"Let me guess," she said. "You already know Billy is harboring a little fugitive in his room." Maggie warmed up her own coffee.

"Guilty as charged. Yeah, I caught on to it. There didn't seem any harm in it. He takes good care of the darn thing, which, by the way, seems smart as a whip. Billy told me that he was warming up to talk to you about it. I thought I'd give him the space to do that. What do you think?" Matt waited for her reply as he finished his coffee.

"You know Billy seriously needs to reattach to things. First, there was the divorce, and then his dad moved away and got remarried. Billy's feeling left behind and angry and just refuses to talk about any of it," she sighed.

"He will, Maggie. Some things take time. You're there for him, and for what it's worth, I let him know I am too. He seemed on the verge of opening up a bit when I caught on to his little secret and gave him some space with it."

"You know Matt; I wish Billy would open up to you more. He's certainly not the happy-go-lucky kid he used to be, and I'm sure there are things he would rather not say directly to me. I have seen a glimmer in the corner of his eye that he likes it when he has your attention."

"Well, now, then there is some progress. Give him time," Matt replied.

"Nothing gets by a mom for long. I went into his room last night, and he had his crazy old Dr. Seuss slipper dug out of the closet. It was sitting on his bed, which seemed odd, and I got curious. When I started to take the slipper off the bed, I saw the mouse sleeping in it as though it had its own little portable bed. It was quite clear to me Billy put the slipper there for a reason, but it was a surprise.

"I don't know. As long as he uses a cage during the day, I don't think anyone would ever know. All I could think was that he should keep it safe, or the exterminator could have it for breakfast. It is cute. It actually rubbed its eyes when I accidentally woke it up. Before the divorce, Billy was promised a pet, and it's been an issue between us. Tough one. I hate to be a rule breaker." Maggie remained in thought with her hands plunged deep into the dishwater.

"It's not as though you went out and bought him the pet. He just happened to find it. Maybe your conscience can squeak by on that note?"

Maggie had to smile. "I love your choice of words. I'll buy into that. I'll tell him over dinner that it's OK. We'll 'Bender the rules' a bit, I guess. But only one mouse. When he was six, he took my wastebasket and collected thirty frogs, which of course, got loose in the house. Do you know how hard it is to find thirty frogs in a shag carpet?"

Matt laughed. "By the way, it's what they call a kangaroo mouse, not an ordinary brown mouse. I looked it up. They're not common around here. If management catches on, offer to pay pet rent. Most complexes have that option."

Maggie nodded.

"Hey, three for supper tonight? I'll bring some cheese. I'm not on duty for the next three days. I'm curious what Billy looks like when he's happy, and finding out he can keep the mouse should make him break down and actually smile." Matt gave Maggie a quick hug and peck on the cheek.

"Yes, to the idea of supper, and you are in for a treat. Billy can be tons of fun. At least he was before he became the Little Lord of Gloom around here."

Matt turned when he reached the door. "By the way, I'm supposed to pick up the heat gun for the Fire Department today. It's our new, fascinating, multi-thousand dollar piece of equipment. We're taking it to Billy's school for a fire prevention presentation, but I bet little Mister Science would enjoy getting a firsthand look at how it works. I'll bring it tonight. It's pretty incredible equipment. You'll be surprised at what it can do. I better get my errands done, and I'll catch a little rest; so I don't fall asleep face down in my supper."

"Sounds good," she called out as he left and closed the door.

Maggie was already thinking about that evening's supper. She jotted down a brief shopping list. Matt had a way about him that made their suppers together the only time she truly relaxed from the pressure she was under. Her workday would probably be ordinary compared to seeing Billy's surprise over the fact that his pet was approved to stay. She delighted in planning how she would tell Billy the news. The tide had to turn at some point, and this might be how things would begin ebbing in the right direction. At the very least, keeping the mouse might put a ripple in the water enough for her to see a bit of genuine happiness leak out of her son.

The Newcomer

Chapter 3

Maggie wiped off the counter and packed up the breakfast garbage. She slipped on her sweater and headed for the door. With no shred of food left out, maybe, she'd return after work to find an ant-free kitchen counter. She hurried as she opened the apartment door and bumped right into the stranger standing on the other side of her door.

"Excuse me." He said with a pleasant boyish smile. "I was just going to knock. I'm Billy's new science teacher, Calvin Phelps. I've been stopping by to meet the other building tenants one by one. I just moved into your building about a month ago."

"Well, welcome to the wonderful world of ants. I was just taking my kitchen trash out, which is what they asked all the tenants to do, while we all wait with bated breath for them to send in an exterminator."

"I hadn't noticed a problem, but I'm single, so I usually don't cook anything. An insect problem surprises me. This is a very nice apartment complex. The matter is that I'm here because Billy mentioned he had a pretty powerful projector microscope. I said I would pick it up and take it to school to show to the class. Billy said it was too large to get on the bus easily." Calvin noticed that Maggie hadn't expected him to stop to pick up the microscope.

Maggie smiled. "At the risk of being only a couple of minutes late for work, in the name of science, I'll take the time to find it. Billy didn't mention it, but if you can wait a minute, I'll get it out of his room. I hate to ask, but can you hold the garbage bag until I get back?"

"No problem. Thanks for the tip about the ants." Calvin stepped into the apartment and quietly closed the door as Maggie departed down the hall to Billy's room.

Calvin silently followed her to the doorway of Billy's bedroom. "Need any help? Wow, nice room. He's got a junior size lab going on in here. I can see you've given Billy a lot of scientific opportunities. He has a reputation for being a science whiz if I can believe what I read in his prior teacher's evaluation notes."

"Billy's adopted. So I'm not sure where all his talents come from, but his interest certainly does seem to gravitate toward science, so my husband, correction, my former husband, and I fostered it ever since he was a tot." Maggie located the microscope behind the bowling game and under the old hockey gear in the closet.

"I hadn't realized Billy's parents were divorced. Not uncommon, I guess, in today's world," Calvin casually added as he moved toward the bed stand next to Billy's bed. From the dark depths in the arm of Calvin's suit coat, six ants silently emerged into the dimly lit room, dropped down on the bed stand, and began traveling toward Billy's closet. Calvin stepped back into the center of the room.

"Here you go." Maggie smiled. "Yep, I've learned divorce lurks where you least expect it. Maybe it would help if you could offer some intriguing extra credit projects for Billy. It just may help end the gloom and doom attitude he's harboring. Billy seems to have lost his enthusiasm for school. It's something I never thought I'd ever see happening."

"It's worth a try. Some sort of recognition in the classroom might help." Calvin exchanged the small bag of trash for the boxed microscope. "Give me a week or so. We'll set up a conference, and then we can talk about any progress he's making."

"Thanks, Mr. Phelps. I think I need an insider at school to help me figure out how to help Billy through all of this. It's been over a year now, and I truly miss the positive side of Billy's personality."

"I'm sure being twelve, you know, the moodiness, and being a new kid trying to fit in, is all part of it. But if you don't mind his having extra homework, I'll try to get him more involved." Calvin carried the box to the door.

"The Science Fair has always been important to Billy, and it's around the time of the year that they begin working on that. Isn't it?" Asked Maggie.

"I noticed he has participated in a science fair before. The students are beginning to select partners for their projects. Does Billy have a second microscope here at home?" Calvin casually asked as he carried the box to the door.

"No. I hope you won't keep it indefinitely. Science is something Billy enjoys. I guess that once curiosity is ignited, there is just no stopping the scientific mind."

Calvin gave Billy's mother a practiced smile, "I only need it until I accomplish what I have set out to do. I shouldn't need it for any extended period."

"No problem, as long as it's back when he starts to work on his science fair project. We might have found an answer or at least the start of renewing Billy's interest in school," Maggie said with a smile.

She felt encouraged after the science teacher left. The day was progressing nicely. She dropped the garbage in the dumpster with enthusiasm. Just the glimmer of hope that progress might be made with Billy's attitude about the new school made the day seem brighter.

Maggie arrived at work a full fifteen minutes late, but she could shave that off her lunch hour and make things right. She was well into her workday, and the pile of clutter had multiplied on her desk when she noticed a telephone message from one of the moms who lived at the complex. The office assistant had scrawled it on the phone message pad. "Maggie, my cell phone just went kaput this morning. So have Julie's, Sandy's, Dot's, and Sue's cell phones. Yours isn't working either. Think we burned them out calling in about the ants? See you later at the phone store in the mall."

Maggie checked her cell phone, and it was dead even on the charger. She had a second charger at home, and she decided to try that one after work.

Having to stand in line at the store and delay tonight's supper didn't sound appealing. The only extra stop she wanted to make on the way home was to pick up Billy and Matt's favorite ice creams. Maggie was determined tonight was reserved for family-style fun. She had off from work the following day. The pet shop and phone store were both at the mall, so those errands could wait until tomorrow.

The Round Table

Chapter 4

Billy slumped over his sheet of art paper. It was white as newly-fallen snow and totally blank. The assignment was to paint an object commonly found at home. He disliked wasting time doing any artwork because he preferred subjects he excelled at. Billy glanced down at the mouse in his pocket and noticed a small loose piece of thread on his shirt. He was on the verge of making two dots on the paper and connecting them when Sarah interrupted his chain of thought.

"Come on, Billy. It's the last day for us to have these done. I'm the table leader, and you're wrecking my score." Sarah was determined to spark Billy into completing the art assignment. She was always trying to experiment with the motivational skills her mother brought home from work. "Simple will have to work for you since you don't have much class time left." She dipped his brush in paint and handed it to him.

"You know, Sarah, art is easy for you. All my artwork is crap. I only do great at science and math." Since the brush already had paint on it, Billy put his brush on the paper and began painting.

"Try quick, short strokes and maybe wavy lines. You don't have to be the best at everything, Billy. Leave some room for the rest of us to excel at our own gifts," Sarah said lightly.

"Is a piece of thread a good idea for this?" Asked Billy. "I'm sure I can handle drawing that."

"Let's try for a little higher grade, Billy." Sarah rolled her eyes, and everyone laughed. "Hey Billy, I got a deal for you. I'm crappy at science, and the Science Fair is coming up pretty soon. If we team up, I bet I can do the art presentation part, and your super brain can win it for us. I'll help with the typing too. How about it?" Sarah watched as he continued his attempts at filling the paper.

Billy was surprised at the offer. Most kids just steered clear of him and his sour attitude since the divorce. The work required for the display boards and typing was always a turn-off about his science fair efforts. "Sure. It's a deal," he said, almost under his breath, and then he was surprised he had agreed.

"That's a shock and a half," said Mae Ling.

"You all heard Mr. Science. We got a deal. Pick any project you like, Billy. Who did you get all that science talent from?" Sarah bantered on while she kept brushes ready for Billy to use. "Your dad or mom must be a super brain. Try some green. Here, use my brush. I'm done already." Sarah decided to grab the opportunity, to chatter away, and get to know her new science partner.

Billy's hand was working the brush while Sarah was hurrying things along by choosing the colors for him and rinsing the brushes out. "I'm adopted," he blurted it out without thinking.

"So am I," said Mae Ling. "Of course, my parents aren't Chinese, so it's no secret. They say it's special because they got to choose me."

Mrs. Wilder, the art teacher, listened quietly at her desk while comments moved around the table like wildfire. Sarah's mother was a corporate motivational speaker, and Sarah was exceptionally skillful at extracting information from other students. Mrs. Wilder thought perhaps what made Billy so glum was about to be revealed. She listened with interest to the table's conversation, waiting to see what Sarah might get the students to disclose.

"I might as well be adopted," Casey said. "My mom and dad just divorced, and who knows what my next father will be like. I already don't like my father's new girlfriend."

Lisa looked depressed for a moment and then added, "My mom says she'll never get married again. Sometimes I wish my dad would come home from where ever the heck he is, but then I don't know how I'd feel about seeing him after five years."

"I'm thinking of going to live with my mom, but I'd have to change schools and make all new friends. My dad spends zero time with me." Kyle felt better letting the truth out.

"Oh Yeah? Well, I could live with just one parent for a change." Lynda sighed. "Mom's getting married for the fourth time, and this guy is the biggest loser of them all. My new stepbrothers are going to be the Schultz twins. That's right. You know the twins that are always sitting in the principal's office?"

Everyone at the table looked wide-eyed at one another.

Mrs. Wilder had the twins in one of her classes. She could not imagine how the two families were going to blend and successfully survive.

"Billy, the secret with Mrs. Wilder is she likes bright colors. Personally, I think it affects our grades. Add some yellow. My dad left two years ago, and it's hard, but we hardly ever saw him. When he was home, my parents argued constantly. I don't think adults are any smarter than kids are about their relationships."

Sarah paused, and then she continued. "How do you like that? Billy's the only one of us with two parents." Sarah was curious to see if Billy would join the conversation.

Billy shifted in his chair. Everyone at the table had problems, but they seemed to be able to talk about them. "Nope, my parents divorced over a year ago. We had to move to an apartment so they could sell the house." The hard truth was he had still been hoping his dad would change his mind, and they'd be a family again. But Billy's dreams met a permanent end when his dad moved to California and started a new family. He felt grateful when the subject under discussion changed.

The art assignment was supposed to feature a household item. Billy took a brush in hand and dipped it in the black paint.

"Wait, Billy! Whatever you're featuring, use red. She likes bright colors. Remember? "Sarah quickly took the black brush and handed him one dipped in red.

"I guess that will work. There are red ants." He drew one red ant in the center of his paper.

"Yeah," said Sarah. That's a household item where I live. Three weeks ago, Mom and I moved over to Countryside Apartments. Really nice apartment but chock full of ants. Mom's upset about it."

"Which building?" Billy blurted out the question before his shyness could edge in to stop him.

"The one next to yours. I saw you walk down to the bus stop this morning. That's when I thought up the offer on the science fair and how I was going to try to rope you into helping me." Sarah smiled brightly over her success, and everyone laughed. Even Billy showed a quick smile.

Mrs. Wilder instructed the class to put their papers on the counter to dry. Billy's red ant immediately caught her attention. During her break time, she decided to make another call to the apartment management, but her cell phone simply didn't work. Now she would have to stop and have it checked on the way home. Ants shouldn't be a household item, but they surely were at her apartment. She could hardly wait until she was out of that complex and living in her new house. After this morning's class, apparently, the only positive thing about her divorce seemed to be that she had no children who had to deal with the breakup of her own marriage.

A Few Puzzle Pieces

Chapter 5

Since the weather had pleasantly warmed, the new science teacher decided to hold class outside. The students welcomed a break from the regular classroom. Mr. Phelps explained various insects and passed around jars of specimens once the students gathered and seated themselves on the grass.

Sarah made sure she took a spot next to Billy. She figured he could be awfully cute if he would just crack a smile once in a while and stop moping around. Now that she had seen him break into that half-smile, he agreed to be her science partner, and they were neighbors, perhaps a friendship was possible with Mr. Super Brain. Lots of kids had shunned her at her old school because of her high grades. For weeks now, Sarah had been enjoying the freedom of pretending she wasn't all that smart. Now she had reached the point where she had to admit she needed a grade level, equal friend.

Billy reached in his pants pocket and dropped two pieces of his morning cereal into his shirt pocket just as Sarah sat down next to him.

Sarah whispered in a low secretive tone. "I thought the brainy geeks carried pen protectors in their shirt pockets. I hate to be the one to tell you, but there's a little mouse hiding in your shirt."

Billy's face flushed. "Hey, please don't say anything. I hate bringing him to school, but I can't leave him home. I don't have a cage, and my mom would find out. You know the rule about no pets?"

"I know," Sarah sighed. "I had to give away my hamster. Hey, I still have the cage. Want to borrow it?"

"That'd be great." Billy felt helpless at the revelation of his secret and had little choice left but to trust Sarah to keep silent about it.

"Maybe he's a lost pet. Sorry to ask, but isn't he going to pee in your pocket?"

"No, it's odd he doesn't, but I always find a chance to sneak off and set him down outside during lunch."

"Maybe he could be part of our science fair project, and then he wouldn't exactly be a pet. Hey, he's peeking at me, or else he's looking at the ant in this jar." Sarah held the jar close to Billy's pocket, and it did look like the mouse was studying the ant intensely.

"My mom has to go to a meeting, so she will be late coming home. We live in building B, number 101. I can give you the cage right after school if you want."

"Thanks, Sarah." Billy broke into the first real grin he'd worn in what seemed ages, and it felt pretty good to him.

"There's a price to pay for the cage. I'd like to hold him for a little while. I miss that darn hamster."

"Yet another deal. Huh, Sarah? OK. That seems fair enough."

"Don't worry, Billy. You can ask anybody. I'm the best at keeping my mouth shut when it comes to secrets."

The class was over, and as Sarah got up to leave, a serious look crossed her face. "I have a science question to ask you when you come over." Billy noticed that for a moment, her face clouded over with uneasiness.

"No problem. See you later," Billy said as he trudged off to his next class. Sarah's offer of her cage had perfect timing to it. It would help a lot since Monday was a gym day. He could leave the Mouse home and not worry that he would get loose and run around the locker room. He could easily find himself sitting in the office with the Shultz twins if that happened. Billy shuddered at the thought.

Billy suddenly realized he felt more sorry for Lynda than he did for himself. "Life isn't perfect, and you just have to do the best with it that you can," he said to Mouse when he stopped at his locker on his way to Math. "Maybe that's what Mom is trying to tell me all the time."

The Burning Question

Chapter 6

The bus groaned to a halt at its customary stop at the complex. As Sarah and Billy walked toward her building, Sarah's mom called her on her cell phone to check how her day at school had gone. Billy no longer had a cell phone. It was one of the extra budget items that no longer existed after the divorce. Billy used any phone handy if he had to call his mom at work. In this case, it was Sarah's.

"Great," said Sarah. "With the parents taken care of, we can execute our secret mission."

"I have to get the cage back into the apartment before the teacher's come home. Mr. Phelps lives in my building. They always stay to do their planners and correct papers, so that will give us a bit of time."

"Mrs. Wilder lives in the building next to me. I bet your painting with the ant on it actually hit home shall we say. That's some pretty smart thinking on that one, Billy. I think you're in for a huge 'A' for artwork on that assignment."

The mouse seemed grateful to get out of the cramped shirt pocket. Billy set him on Sarah's kitchen table and gave him the rest of the cereal and the piece of cheese. He put a paper towel down on the floor in case the mouse had to pee.

Sarah returned with a small cage complete with a water bottle and exercise wheel. "Wow. You weren't kidding. You are a super-brain with a super-brain mouse. My hamster sure wasn't potty trained. Hey, look. He's got long feet like a little kangaroo."

"I see what you mean," said a rather puzzled Billy. I've only had him a week, and he catches on to everything. I'm trying to figure that one out. Maybe you're right. We need to make him part of the science fair project. I'm sure I can think up something interesting."

"What's his name?"

"I haven't given him a real name yet." Billy looked at her sheepishly. "I fell asleep in front of the fireplace watching TV, and when I woke up, he was sitting on my leg. It looked really funny. He was sitting there swinging his tail and watching the news. I called to him, "Hey, Mouse! Come over here." Billy shrugged. "I mean, what else was I supposed to call him? He came right over to me and sat down in front of me on the couch. It just seems to me that he likes the name Mouse."

Sarah sat down at the table and called to the mouse. To her surprise, he came right to her. "Not creative, but he does like the name. It works, so don't change it. Mouse it is. But if you can teach him to talk, all's fair if he calls you Boy," she said with a smile.

Sarah tickled the mouse behind the ears. "He has intense and intelligent eyes. My hamster had the attention span of a flea." She got up and went to the fridge to get a bottle of juice they could share. "Oh no, not again. Billy, come over here and look at this."

Billy went over to the kitchen counter where she stood. Seven small ants were picking up toast crumbs and carrying them while one carpenter-type ant paced and hovered over them. While they watched, they noticed that as sturdy and strong looking as the larger ant was, it did not bother helping with the crumbs the others were struggling to carry. Billy could see the big ant's antenna rapidly whipping around. "Watch the big one closely. It seems like he's giving the other ants orders or something. They communicate with their antennas.

"Want to see something really crazy?" Billy brought the mouse over to the counter. "Go get them, Mouse." The words were barely spoken when the mouse stomped on all the crumb carriers.

"I don't believe it! Look at his feet fly! Maybe you ought to rename him Kung Fu, Charlie." Sarah's laughter immediately began to fade.

Oddly enough, the mouse began gnashing his teeth as he slowly edged around the larger ant, and the ant was slowly backing away. "What the heck?" Billy muttered under his breath.

The mouse forced the ant to back up against the counter wall, turned, and smacked the ant hard with its tail. The mouse let out a squeal, but the ant was neither crushed nor fazed by the blow.

"Billy, whatever you do, don't let that ant escape. I've got to catch it." Sarah ran from the room and came back with a small glass jar and a pair of tweezers. The mouse had hit the ant again with his tail, but once again, that failed to have any effect on the ant.

Sarah seized the ant with the tweezers and put it in the jar, quickly screwing the lid on tight. "Boy, those tweezers got hot awfully fast. Come on, Billy, let's see if I'm right." She motioned for Billy to follow her into the bathroom. "Flip off the lights." Once Billy flipped the light switch, both of them watched in total darkness.

Sarah shook the jar hard and then held it up. In the eerie darkness of the bathroom, the ant glowed a bright red. "Success," said Sarah. We've got ourselves one red hot ant."

They took the jar back to the kitchen. The mouse was sitting on the counter among the scattered bodies of the other dead ants. It was quietly licking its tail.

Sarah went over to the mouse. "Poor thing, I bet I know what's wrong with you." Sure enough, there were two burn marks on the mouse's tail. Sarah pulled some burn cream out of her backpack and smoothed it on the mouse's injured tail.

"I know it doesn't seem to make any sense Billy, but neither does this." Sarah rolled up her shirt sleeve. She had at least a dozen angry burn marks, each large as the ant they had captured in the jar.

"Those look awful," Billy said. "They're even partly blistered."

"This was what I wanted to talk to you about," Sarah continued. What kind of ant burns instead of biting?

"I'm no expert, but it doesn't sound probable," said Billy, still looking at the burn marks on her arm.

"I woke up two nights ago, and red glow-in-the-dark ants were on my arm. I thought I was dreaming at first until I felt the pain. The minute I moved, the ants seared my arm like a steak on a grill. It was so painful my mom took me to see the doctor. I explained it to the Doctor, but he acted like I was pretty darn crazy. I think he thought I burned myself with something on purpose. He said it would be helpful if I could catch one since he'd never seen insect bites like that. Now that I have one of the ants, he can put it on his own arm and see I was being truthful. Besides, both of us saw how Mouse got the burns on his tail. I really feel sorry for Mouse. Mine still really hurt, and his must too."

"It seems to be a defensive action on the ant's part," mused Billy. "They go into some sort of attack mode when threatened."

"We can look at it under my projection microscope," said Billy. "Darn it. My microscope is at school in the science lab. Mr. Phelps brought it in for me today."

"The school's still open," Sarah reminded him.

"Right," said Billy. "I'm going to head back to school and get it. It'll enlarge the ant, and then I can get a decent look at it. Can I use your phone to call my mom again?"

"Sure, call her. But I want to see what it looks like too. After all, I am one of its victims. Maybe, if he's still at school, we can ask Mr. Phelps what kind of ant he thinks this is. It'll help the exterminators figure out what they're up against."

"If they ever get here," said Billy. "I hope no one is just sitting waiting for them to arrive. We've had a lot of the small ants for weeks now, which is what everybody has been complaining about and getting no management response. The red hot ants are a more dangerous problem. Maybe we can figure out an amazing science project out of all this."

Maggie was delighted to hear enthusiasm back in her son's voice. The fact that he had made a new friend from their apartment complex delighted her. She agreed to pick them up and gave them a full two and a half hours to get back to school and do their work in the science lab. She let Billy know her cell phone wasn't working, so any phone calls had to be made to the office and before she left for home.

Mouse had been sitting on the table intently watching the ant continuously ram itself against the side of the glass jar. Sarah took the jar and dropped it in her backpack, and Billy tucked Mouse back into his shirt pocket.

They slipped on their backpacks and headed over to bury the cage deep in Billy's closet for the time being.

Sarah's Confession

Chapter 7

"Whoa," said Sarah as they walked into Billy's room.

"Mom must have pulled everything half out of the closet digging out the microscope this morning. I forgot to tell her Mr. Phelps was going to pick it up. Sorry. I'm usually pretty orderly." Billy put the cage in the back of the closet and began piling his old hockey equipment, shoes and games back in the closet on top of it.

Sarah was immediately fascinated with the Junior Science lab equipment. Billy had a couple of pieces of advanced equipment. At first, she carefully concealed the fact that she knew what she saw there. She'd lost friends before by competing too much. If she was ever going to get to share using his lab, she decided it was better if Billy caught onto the fact that she also excelled in math and science.

"Beakers, funnels, a ring stand, test tube racks, and your mom lets you use a Bunsen Burner in your bedroom?" Sarah asked.

"Only since I was eight," Billy added. "You like that kind of stuff?"

"It's part of what I call my past life," Sarah sighed. "Oh, look here. You even keep a notebook. My dad did that. I remember him from when I was small. He let me look in it, but then things changed."

"How so?" Billy asked as he stuffed the last items in the closet.

"Well, when I was small, he used to let me sit up on a stool and watch him in his home lab, and I truly liked that. But then he went to work for a different research firm and moved all his science equipment there. They started to send him on trips to Europe. Mom hated that, and the trips went on for months sometimes. We never went with him. Mom worked for an art auction house as a buyer back then, so she couldn't drop everything and go. After a few years, she finally did ask to go with him, and then he told her that he didn't want us with him on the trips."

"What was he researching?" Billy asked her.

"Mom says he refused to discuss it. She's right because I remember listening to the two of them arguing. My mom is kind of strange. She gets involved in her own work and doesn't pay much attention to family things. When she finally did ask questions, my dad claimed it was a government contract, and he was not supposed to discuss it. He did call home sometimes while he was on his trips, and he sent her money." Sarah hesitated for a moment. "But he left for Switzerland two years ago and, well, the calls and money stopped. We don't think that he ever got there. He just disappeared off the face of the earth."

"Gee, Sarah. How awful for you," Billy said.

"So far, we can't find out anything, so Mom and I just have to wait for news, and as Mom says to just go on with life. It's hard not knowing, but he had become like a stranger to us over those few years. Mom spends a lot of time away, and my Uncle is the one who picks up the pieces for me and spends the most time with me."

"That's a tough one, Sarah." Billy couldn't help but feel sympathy for her situation. "Do you even know what your dad's research specialty was?"

"Genetics. It's like I had a dad, but then he slowly vaporized. He didn't even leave me a beaker to remember him by because he moved his lab out of the house. There are just a few photos of when I was little. As my Mom says, all we have left of him is the same mysterious brown triangle in my left eye that tells the world I was his daughter."

Billy froze on the spot for a second. "I'm sorry that happened to you."

"I'm sorry if I said too much," Sarah said. It was apparent that she was feeling a bit embarrassed.

"Sarah? Look at me a minute."

When Sarah turned and faced him, both of them realized that not only was their eye color nearly identical, but each of their left eyes had the same small brown triangle.

"I guess the chances of a brown triangle happening are more frequent than I thought." They both said at once.

"Maybe it's just the mark of exceptional math and science aptitude," Billy ventured.

"All this time, I thought it was the one thing I had left from my father. Go figure. I guess we can research that one after we figure out what's up with the red hot ants," Sarah answered as she slipped on her backpack. "OK. I admit it. I'm terrific at math too. My days of faking average grades at school are over. In a way, it's a relief being honest and just to be me."

"Come on, Sarah, let's complete our mission." Billy assumed if the lab were locked, the janitor would open it up just long enough to use his microscope.

Firm Resolve

Chapter 8

Billy was silent as they hiked back to school. Nothing about the ants made any sense. At least he felt comfortable to know Mouse was safe and curled up in his pocket.

"What's your take on all of this, Billy?" Sarah hoped Billy had assembled the facts and arrived at some conclusion about the strange ant behavior.

"I'm pretty stumped. Carpenter ants are the same size, but they gnaw on wood. This puts a new twist on fire ants for sure. They bite and use venom and are pretty small. Maybe these have escaped from a lab experiment, but anyway you cut it, it's no laughing matter. I can't believe what they did to your arm!"

"Maybe now the doctor and my mother will stop thinking I'm crazy. Although, I guess I would think that too if I hadn't seen it with my own eyes. I meant to ask you, did you teach your mouse to kill ants?"

"Nope. It beats me why he does it," Billy answered with a shrug.

"I had high hopes that someday I could recommend you to Columbia Pictures for a job as the world's greatest animal wrangler."

"With my vast fortune, I'd build my apartment complex with a rule that the tenants all had to have pets." Their laughter was a welcome relief from their anxiety. They hurried down the street, needing to get back to the lab before the school closed for the day.

"Brother, who knows how many of these ants are in the buildings," Sarah said with a perplexed look on her face. "All the ones in my room that night got away, so there are around a dozen at least likely still there. Any way you cut it, those ants need to go. There has to be a way to find them and kill them. Now that we have one, we can find out what kind they are. So we are making some progress. Right?"

"We also found out they come out during the day and also at night," Billy remarked as he added a little more speed to his step.

"I don't care if they are on the endangered species list. After what the ants did to me, I consider a dozen an infestation. Maybe that kind of ant is only in my apartment. Race you," Sarah said as they neared the school.

"Or maybe," thought Billy, "all the carpenter size ants we've been seeing are red hot ants." He felt sick at the thought of it. Maybe the larger ant on his sandwich yesterday came from the cafeteria. That could mean the school is infested. What stuck in his head and kept nagging him for an explanation was the behavior of the larger ant toward the small ants and, beyond that, the mouse's strange tactics in trying to kill the larger ant.

It seemed as if the mouse knew that kind of ant was downright dangerous.

They dashed up the school steps, down the hall, and around the corner to the lab door. They still had almost an hour before their school closed.

Juggling the Jar

Chapter 9

The halls were quiet, and the science lab was empty. Sarah and Billy pulled up a couple of chairs in front of the back table where the projection microscope was still plugged in.

She pulled the glass jar out of her backpack. They saw that the ant was still ramming at the glass walls of the jar with its head.

"Hey, hot head, feeling a little bit of anger, are you? Well, so am I, after those burns on my arm. We are about to see what you are all about. I guess it didn't need much air because it's still going and glowing red hot. How are we going to do this, Billy?"

"You said the tweezers got hot, so put on a glove. Hold the thing tight under the lens of the scope. I'll need your cell phone to take a picture of what we see. Whatever happens, don't let it get away!"

"Billy, could you hold it and let me take the picture? I can't tell how hard I'm squeezing the tweezers with the glove on."

"Yeah, OK. The glove's too bulky for you. I got him. Wow. I'm squeezing hard enough to split him in two, and he just keeps squirming around." Sarah and Billy both stared into the jar.

Sarah cranked up the magnification while Billy held the ant under the scope.

"What the heck? Do you see that, Sarah? It looks robotic up close! It's obviously made of some kind of metal!"

Sarah snapped a couple of photos of the image on the microscope screen. The ant continued trying to squirm free, but Billy held it firmly in the tweezers.

A voice that sounded like a low, quaking, rasping growl came from across the room and behind them. "What do you two think you're doing? You have no permission to be in the lab."

Sarah sprang up and turned, knocking her chair between her and the enraged science teacher. It was Mr. Phelps, alright, but certainly not the mild-mannered teacher that taught their class earlier that day. He staggered toward her, his reddened face contorting and seething with anger.

"Get it in my jar," Sarah whispered to Billy. He dropped the ant into her jar, and Sarah quickly twisted the cap on to seal it. Mr. Phelps' shaking hands were twisted like claws, but he could still move them swiftly. He made a grab for the jar, but Sarah was too fast for him.

"It's not one of your specimens. It's mine!" Sarah cried out as she backed up against the wall. She was about to drop the jar into her backpack when Mr. Phelps snarled and grabbed the backpack from her. Sarah tossed the jar to Billy, who caught it in mid-air. She promptly dived under the table and slid out the other side.

Mr. Phelps spun around. His eyes were bulging, and his mouth was hideously twisted. The teacher staggered closer and spoke in an unearthly high-pitched scream, "Give me that jar." The strange pitch of his voice sent a shock wave of fear through Billy.

He flung a chair between himself and Mr. Phelps, who momentarily stumbled backward.

Sarah was now six feet behind Billy. He tossed the jar back to her and yelled, "Just run, Sarah." Sarah sped to the doorway, but she had no intention of leaving Billy behind in the lab with a teacher who was way out of control. Mr. Phelps was reeling and only a distorted rendition of himself.

Billy ripped the electric cord out of the wall and grabbed his scope off the table. He saw the teacher's veins protruding and throbbing on his neck and face. The teacher was covered with dripping sweat. In a panic, Billy gave a chair a hard kick. It slid straight into the knees of the approaching Mr. Phelps. The teacher staggered into the display table. Insect specimen jars sailed through the air and scattered to the floor, spinning and rolling in every direction. Billy gave Sarah's backpack a quick kick to propel it to the doorway, and she quickly scooped it up.

They both raced like the wind down the hall and out the entrance to the school. The janitor came sprinting down the hall, yelling for them to stop, but they had never hesitated while they ran for the school door. It seemed only a few split seconds, and Billy and Sarah were nearly three blocks away. They finally ducked into a yard and stopped to catch their breath.

Under Cover

Chapter 10

Billy and Sarah had slipped into the side of a yard where there were plenty of bushes to provide cover. They leaned against a large tree, shaking and taking the time to catch their breath.

"Did I really see what I just saw?" Sarah finally asked. "What the heck happened, and what was that all about? Was that Mr. Phelps or not?" Sarah's face reflected fear and confusion, but mostly total disbelief.

"That was like being inside a fright night movie, and they sure did a good job at casting the teacher," Billy answered. "That was beyond believing, but we both saw it happen. I would say that Mr. Phelps just earned himself a failing grade for after-class conduct."

Sarah was breathing deeply, trying to stabilize herself. "Maybe correcting the Schultz twins' test papers finally got to him," Sarah said with a weak smile.

"Right about now, I can say I'll pass on an invitation to stay after school. Things were pretty crazy. Sarah, just shove it all out of your head, for now, so we can think straight."

Sarah nodded.

"We better not wait here or at school for my mom. We can cut across to the church parking lot from here. I've got a funny feeling that we better not dare get back to the apartments before my mom does because he might be waiting for us. But first off, I'll bet he will probably be checking the streets for us. Are you OK now?"

Sarah shook her head in agreement. "Yeah, if he spots us, and he's in his car, let's not forget that he's over the edge already. I'll bet he could get a case of road rage pretty easily. Billy, this is just downright insane."

They crossed the street and ducked behind the church just as a group of guys were gathering to start a street hockey game. Billy stuffed the scope under the stairs out of sight. He reached in his pocket. The mouse seemed fine but extremely grateful to stretch his legs.

Sarah sat down on the stairs, rummaged in her backpack, and slipped a hooded sweatshirt over her head. "My orange shirt is a dead giveaway even at a distance." She jammed her hair up and under the baseball cap she had pulled out of her backpack. The mouse sat down by Sarah's shoe and began checking the burns on its tail.

"You're right. Good thinking." Billy pulled a windbreaker out of his backpack and slipped it on. "You're going to have to keep Mouse in your front pocket. Just don't forget he's in there. OK?" Sarah looked for the mouse and saw it sitting by

Billy's backpack, chattering and gnashing its teeth. The mouse calmed down when Sarah picked it up, and she tucked it in her hand warmer pocket. Billy tossed their backpacks under the stairs.

"Mouse was clicking his teeth nonstop all the time we were hassling with Mr. Phelps. While he was in my pocket, I could feel it continue. Go figure that one." Billy shrugged.

"Well, I guess this is what they call going undercover," Billy said. "Come on, Sarah. We have to talk, but it's time to make ourselves inconspicuous." They headed over towards the game that had started. Billy picked up two hockey sticks lying in the grass. He handed off one of them to Sarah. "Here, hold it in front of you and sort of lean on it and watch the game, so we look like part of the group."

One of the players called over, "Hey, you two want in the game?"

"See you in a couple of minutes," Billy yelled back.

"Billy, I've got to admit this whole thing is pretty scary to me. Part of me says it couldn't be true or have happened. It doesn't make any sense for a teacher to act like that. He was like a robotic monster. I can wait forever before I have to face science class Monday." Sarah swayed back and forth like Billy and kept her head low with the brim of her baseball cap covering her face.

"I'm sure we're in a heap of trouble. The only pluses are that we still have your ant and the microscope to examine it some more."

"Actually, it was Mr. Phelps that caused all the problems. It was my ant and your microscope."

"Yeah, but when those specimen jars started rolling around and breaking, I have to admit I did take something out of the lab. A jar rolled out of somewhere or other with five ants in it. I've got it in my backpack. Maybe they're just regular old ants, but now I feel like I desperately need to be sure. Wow. As I recall, we were going to ask him for help. I think not. Sorry, but we only have ourselves to trust to get to the bottom of this."

"Somehow, someway," said Sarah. "We will figure out what's going on."

They both recognized Mr. Phelps Volvo as it began to cruise the church parking lot. It was moving so slowly that there was no mistake that he was trying to see if he could spot Billy and Sarah.

Sarah gave Billy a quick glance that was laced with fear.

"Don't run, and don't lose it now. Nothing could be as strange as what we saw. Come on," said Billy. They made their way into the thick of a group of players who were taking a water break.

Billy walked up to the guy who had called over to him. "Hey, our group got shut out of playing at the Countryside complex. Bad accident with a dumpster."

"Yeah, I heard. Well, you can bring the guys over here. We could use more players, and I'm sure it'll be OK with Father McCully. He plays with us most of the time. Got your own goalie, I hope? Truth be known, we wear ours out good and proper. My name's Jimmy, but they call me Jimmy the Stick."

"Yeah. Then I guess you can call me Billy the Goalie. We have nine, maybe ten players, and maybe three are pretty slick."

Billy could see the Volvo had stopped, and the driver seemed to be watching the players.

"We can hit the lot any day of the week except when Father needs it for a parking lot. Just go stop to see him, and he'll fill you in. Father is cool. He played ice hockey at St. Joe's. He's a priest, but he's into any kind of hockey. He's hoping we get enough players to have a hockey church festival. You can even store your net here if you want to. She plays too?" Jimmy motioned toward Sarah.

Jimmy didn't say it in a negative way, so Sarah piped in, "Nope, but I can learn to keep score if you need help with that."

"Talk to Father. He would rather play with us, but he usually ends up having to keep score and get things organized. I sure bet he'd love some help."

Sarah acted casual while she watched the Volvo turn around. It began making its way out of the parking lot and out onto the street. She nodded to Billy.

Billy took a couple more minutes to wrap up the conversation just to be sure that the coast was definitely clear. "We'll be back on Saturday to get things arranged," he finally told Jimmy.

They left the sticks where they had found them, grabbed the gear they had stowed under the stairs, then cut through a few backyards while heading toward the complex.

It seemed a smart idea to stay out of sight, so they headed toward the apartment clubhouse, but they quickly spotted the Volvo cruising around the parking lot there. They hung back toward the hiking area by the edge of the woods. Billy found a spot where they could see his mom pull into the place she usually parked.

They were still within the time frame Billy's mom had given them, but it was time to call her and change the plan.

Billy dialed her work number. "Mom, it's me. I got done early. Are you coming straight home because I've got a big surprise for you?"

"Sure I can. I'm leaving now, but I have one quick stop to make. I should be there in twenty minutes or so. A big surprise, huh?"

"Yeah, it's a huge one. So can you promise to wait in the car until I get there?"

"Ok. You know I positively love surprises. Love you. See you in a bit. By the way, don't forget you can't call my cell phone. Something's wrong with it. So no more changes in your plans."

"Got it," Billy said and hung up. Billy and Sarah looked at each other. Billy rolled his eyes. "Well, the big surprise isn't the half of it, and I know for sure it's not the kind of surprise my mom will truly enjoy."

"Or mine. That'll be a new one for Mom. I've never, ever gotten into trouble." Sarah looked a bit apprehensive.

"It almost seems like the older you get, the more confusing moments you have and the easier it is to get into trouble. Actually, it's nothing I want to get into regularly." Billy added. "Don't worry, Sarah. They usually go easy on first-time offenders."

"You never realize how safe you feel until you suddenly aren't," Sarah mused. "It doesn't help that what we have to tell them is beyond belief."

A Taste of Discipline

Chapter 11

Calvin Phelps pulled the Volvo over on the shoulder of the service road in a secluded area of the park. He'd done his duty and searched up and down the streets, and everywhere kids were hanging out. He'd patrolled the streets, the complex, the clubhouse, and even the church parking lot. Billy and Sarah, somehow, seemed to have evaporated into thin air and successfully eluded him. He knew that sooner or later, they would both have to return to the apartment complex. After all, they had to go home. The problem was once they did return home, then others would be involved. Calvin doubted the two of them had gone to the police for help. They were just kids, and even if they did, their story would sound so unlikely that nothing would be investigated.

He shivered. His clothes were soaked with the sweat that poured off of him relentlessly. Calvin could feel the onset of the oncoming changes. The pulsating rhythm of his heart began surging through every inch of his body until he jerked with each beat. The fevered pitch of a continual whine in his ears would soon set in. Calvin desperately struggled to brace himself against the oncoming pain he knew he was about to be dealt. The sound would increase in decibels until it seared every cell of his brain.

Calvin understood he was about to be disciplined. He had suffered the effects before. From the moment he saw Sarah and Billy in the lab bent over the microscope, with one of the ants in a jar, the force had taken control of him. He grasped at piecing together why he should be considered directly responsible for any minor interference that two children possibly could create.

It was quite possible; they had not looked at the ant under the microscope yet. He'd done his part to get the microscope out of Billy's possession before the scheduled events unfolded. No matter how bright those two students were, it was unlikely they could stop the agenda which had been carefully planned. Things had already begun to unfold.

Calvin felt blameless and undeserving of being the recipient of such intense pain, but that didn't change his situation. His brain felt hotter, and the decibels began to increase.

"Please, make it stop so I can think," he sobbed and pleaded. He was vaguely aware of a revised plan being inserted and developing somewhere in his brain. But his reasoning was disjointed and disrupted by the escalating level of the piercing sounds. It became impossible for him to chain any thoughts together.

An ominous silence suddenly came over him. The excruciating mental noise was suspended for a few moments. Every nerve in his body clung desperately to the hope that the throbbing whine would not resume. He collapsed behind the steering wheel. When he resumed consciousness, it was almost nightfall. The plan was now clearly fixed in his head. Now he knew what he was expected to do.

True Confessions

Chapter 12

Billy and Sarah spotted his mother's car as soon as it rolled into her parking space.

"Here goes," Billy said, steeling himself. "What we have to explain is nothing short of the unbelievable, but we do have evidence."

Maggie saw the two of them rushing over to her car. "Well, hi there," she said to Sarah. "You must be Julie's daughter. You look a lot like her."

"Yeah, Mrs. Bender, I am," Sarah said quietly. Then she quickly blurted out, "I'm so sorry. I got Billy in some trouble at school, but I certainly didn't mean to."

"Oh, that kind of surprise," Maggie said. "Maybe we should all sit down and talk about it." As she got out of the car, Maggie noticed the two of them seemed in a huge hurry to reach the door to the apartment building.

While Maggie went to change out of her work clothes, Sarah and Billy sat down at the kitchen table. Sarah set the mouse on her lap. She whispered in a low voice to Billy. "Explaining about having a mouse is small potatoes compared to all that has happened. Right now, I feel lucky that my mom is going to be home late tonight."

"After all that bizarre stuff, it sure feels better with a parent around. You shouldn't take the blame for what happened. One thing led to another, and somehow it all got out of control." Billy fell silent, trying to figure out where to begin explaining it all.

As Maggie came back into the kitchen, a sudden knock at the door caused Billy and Sarah to freeze in their chairs momentarily.

It was Matt. "Hey, I came over early to help make supper." He set a grocery bag on the counter and gave Maggie a quick kiss on the cheek. "Whoa, I walked in on something or other, didn't I?" Matt said as he looked at Billy and Sarah sitting nervously at the table. "Family party, or can I join in?"

"Hi, Uncle Matt," Sarah said with a half-smile. "I'm awfully glad you're here. We, ah, got in some trouble after school, and we were just going to try to explain it all."

"You got into trouble? That's hard to believe. Your mother called me late this afternoon and explained she was coming home pretty late. She asked that I take care of your supper. I was just going over to the apartment to round you up." There was still a touch of foreboding in the air. It implied to Matt that the trouble after school wasn't just a small, fleeting matter.

Maggie knew they all needed time to discuss things, so she quickly agreed, "Let's make it four for supper then. All you're in for is soup and grilled sandwiches. Well, fire away kids while we put the meal together." Billy had given her little trouble in the past. Maggie quietly reassured herself this problem couldn't be all that bad.

Sarah took a deep breath. She had made up her mind to shift the blame on herself since she had never been in any trouble before. She took advantage of the fact that Billy was hesitating and searching to find the right words.

Sarah began summing things up. "Billy and I decided to team up for a science fair project. When we first got home, we stopped over at my building, saw some ants, and captured one of the big ones. Since Billy's projector microscope was at school, we went back there to examine the ant to see what kind it was."

Maggie said, "Darn it, here they come again," as she swiped two small ants up with a paper towel. "Go on. Sorry to interrupt."

Billy noticed Sarah had wisely left the mouse out of the explanation for the moment. He intervened. "Sarah, show them what the carpenter size ants did to your arm."

Sarah pulled off her sweatshirt and rolled up her sleeve.

Matt gave a low whistle as he and Maggie looked at the dozen burn marks. "Are you sure ants did this?" Maggie and Matt couldn't believe what they saw.

"My mom took me to the doctor. They're burns, not bites. The ants came into my room the other night. I don't know what kind they are, but they glow red in the dark, get hot, and burn you. See, I have one that we captured in a jar." Sarah slipped the jar out of her backpack and put it on the table. The ant was showing plenty of angry agitation. "We hoped to ask Mr. Phelps what kind of ant it was if he was at the lab."

"It should be dead by now. There are no air holes in the lid," Billy added. "You can't crush it. I know this is hard to believe, but when we looked at it close up under the scope, it looks like a little metal robot."

Sarah flipped open her cell phone and showed Matt and Maggie the photos she had taken of the ant while it was under the microscope.

Matt picked up the jar and peered at the ant through the glass. Were you able to ask the science teacher about it?"

"That's just it," Billy continued. "Mr. Phelps suddenly showed up in the lab and saw us there. He went absolutely crazy trying to get the ant away from us."

"Crazy in what way?" Asked Maggie.

"His voice was strange," Sarah said. "He was sweating and shaking, and his face was all twisted up. It was downright scary how threatening he looked, and he was trying to take my ant away from me. I told him that it was an ant I found, not one from his jars, but he kept coming after me." Sarah was quite shaken up recalling the situation. "Billy shoved some chairs at him, and he tripped and fell and broke a lot of his insect specimen jars."

Billy looked at his mom with wide-eyed honesty written on his face. "After that happened, I did take this one jar that came rolling at me. It had five live ants in it, and I wanted to compare them. Honestly, that's all I took from the lab: just one jar and my own scope."

"Maybe the teacher had some kind of seizure," Matt interjected.

"I don't think so because after we left school, Mr. Phelps came looking for us in his car," Sarah said. "We ducked into the group of kids playing hockey at the church so that he couldn't spot us, and then we ran back here."

"Here's the jar I took from the lab." Billy pulled his backpack up on the table. He took out his gym shorts and several books. "Oh no," he hesitated. Something must have happened when I threw my backpack under the stairs by the church."

The glass jar was on the bottom of Billy's backpack, but it had broken into several large pieces.

The Metal Detective

Chapter 13

"Billy, don't reach in the bag," Sarah quickly warned him.

"Maybe you should shake it out on the tile floor," Maggie suggested.

As the remaining contents tumbled out of the backpack onto the kitchen floor, Billy hesitated to believe what he saw and then sighed with relief. "They are trapped by the power of my earth magnet. Another piece of proof the ants are actually made of metal!"

"Let's get them in a jar; I don't trust them. Use a potholder," exclaimed Sarah. Maggie grabbed an empty plastic jar and used an oven glove to pick up the magnet and drop it into the jar.

The mouse was still sitting on Sarah's lap, but the moment the ants were dumped out of the backpack, he began his low warning chatter.

Sarah glanced helplessly at Billy and tried to quiet the mouse by petting it.

"What's that strange noise?" Maggie asked.

Sarah's eyes got larger. "It might be my stomach, Mrs. Bender."

Billy looked closely at the squirming ants that were stuck to the magnet. "You better find a glass jar, Mom, because I can already see little dents forming in the plastic. It looks like their temperature is on the rise. They must be able to control how hot they get because, for some reason, they didn't burn their way out of my backpack."

Billy used a wooden-handle knife to quickly scrape the ants into the glass jar from his magnet. "My earth magnet looks like a pretty decent weapon to use against them. Let's not leave it in the jar. I wonder where Mr. Phelps found these. He lives in the complex, but he told the class that he caught most of his insects at school."

"Well, the ants are in the jar, and supper is ready. Let's sit down to eat and try to figure out what's going on." Sarah quickly got up to help Maggie and motioned to Billy toward the kitchen counter. The mouse was sitting by the sink.

Billy looked at Sarah and gave a helpless shrug.

Billy broke the thoughtful silence during the meal. "I have a metal detector. Maybe we could use it to check Sarah's room because the red hot ants that burned her might still be there."

Matt took his cell phone out of his pocket. "Sam has a large construction magnet that collects nails and screws off the ground. I'll borrow it, and we can check out Sarah's apartment and this one. I'll call him.

"By the way, Maggie, your cell phone was down earlier today. Is it back up working? Now mine looks like it has gone dead." He tapped it firmly a couple of times on the table, and an ant tumbled out of the charger receptacle. "What the heck?" Matt turned his empty glass upside down and trapped the ant underneath it. He reached over to the cupboard and grabbed Maggie's cell phone. After several taps, an ant shot across the table. Matt quickly slid the overturned glass over to Billy, who captured the loose ant.

"There's quite a few of my friends that just had their cell phones go down. I wonder if ..." Before Maggie could finish, seemingly from nowhere, Mouse jumped on the table and began chattering and circling the upside-down drinking glass. The mouse seemed to be looking for a fight. The ants were ramming against the glass as though they were challenging him in retaliation.

Billy had to hold his hand on top of the glass because Mouse began kicking at it in a frenzy. Mouse was definitely trying to knock the glass over and get at the ants.

"I think he's mad because his tail got burned when we captured the ant in my kitchen." Sarah hesitated for a moment. She noticed everyone's eyes riveted on the confrontation between the ants and the mouse. "Mouse has unusual reactions to things. That's why we seriously need him for our science fair project."

Billy took his cue from Sarah's comment. He used his earth magnet to snag the two additional ants and add them to the glass jar. "Mom, I, uh, have been sort of, ah, waiting to talk to you about keeping Mouse. We found out he knows how to help us find the ants, and believe it or not; he can recognize if they're the dangerous ones or not."

Now that the ants were contained in the jar, the mouse calmed down and hopped over to Billy.

"Well, the crackers and cereal I found in your laundry for the last week gave me a clue. Once I saw him sleeping in your old slipper on your bed, it made sense. It wasn't hard to figure it out, Billy." Maggie began gathering up the dishes and rinsing them off.

"Sarah lent me her hamster cage. That's why we went over to her apartment after school. Mom, will you think about letting me keep him?"

"As long as he can stay out of trouble while we're not home, I'm willing to give a pet a try."

"Thanks, Mom. You're the best." Billy's face lit up with his old, familiar smile.

Maggie laughed. "You owe me at least one of those smiles every day, or the mouse staying is in serious jeopardy. Let's at least try to keep it low-key about having a pet in the apartment."

"It's a deal," said Billy sighing with relief.

Matt got up from the table. "I think Sam should be home by now, so I'll nab his magnet. I have the heat detector gun from the fire department in my truck. If the metal detector doesn't register, the heat gun is extremely sensitive to even minor temperature elevations. Hopefully, we can detect the location of the ants. Maybe you two want to do the dishes, but Billy and I have some serious detective work to do. If the mouse is a terrific little "metal detective," we can use all the help we can get."

Sarah and Maggie looked at one another, and Maggie exclaimed, "Oh no, the dishes can wait. We want in on searching for the ants!"

The Search Begins

Chapter 14

Billy got up from the table. "I think we need to know a little more about this enemy. Let's take the jar somewhere dark and see just how red hot we can get them to glow." He headed for the bathroom, and everyone followed him down the hall.

Once the flip of the light switch entirely darkened the room, Billy's voice broke the silence. "It's my guess they can control their own individual temperature, but if they get agitated, it causes a physiological reaction which automatically increases their body temperature. If they practice insect-type thinking, it's likely a chain reaction occurs." The ants in the jar had a faint red glow, but when Billy kept slapping the jar with the flat of his hand, the ants became agitated, and their color quickly changed to a bright red, illuminating the jar.

The mouse chattered away on Billy's shoulder. In the darkness, they saw that five more ants were on the sink counter. They began glowing as red as the ants which were captured in the jar.

Billy whistled low under his breath. "They might be little robots, but they sure are communicating with each other." Billy flipped the light on and swept up the ants with his earth magnet, and scraped them into the jar.

Billy tested his metal detector. It was working, but it did not prove sensitive enough when checked against Sarah's jar, which still held only one ant.

Matt brought in the heat detector gun. It showed a heat path by the mirror's edge where the mouse had been checking for more ants. Mouse seemed as reliable as the heat gun when it came to locating the ants.

They decided to go to Sarah's apartment and check it first. They felt there was a strong possibility that the ants that had burned Sarah's arm might still be there. Matt stopped at Sam's apartment and borrowed the nail magnet.

They hurried along the sidewalk towards Sarah's apartment building. Maggie thought out loud, "I don't understand why they would crawl into the cell phones."

"All I can think is that they might be hitching a ride in order to spread to new locations," Billy surmised.

Sarah's voice wavered, "If they came from the school, who knows how many phones they got into and how many locations they went to."

Maggie shuddered at the thought.

"Let's not jump to conclusions. I sure hope that's not the case," Matt said as he looked over at Billy. "If we can locate them, that's only part of the battle. We still have to figure out how to get rid of them for good."

No Time to Waste

Chapter 15

The master plan had been changed. The details of the modified agenda were now shaped in Calvin Phelp's mind and firmly locked in place. There was no longer time to release the ants, a few at a time. A low-pitched whine in his ears assured him that time was of the essence. Calvin began to sweat once again. It was a reminder that he had better follow the instructions to the very last letter. Failure of the mission meant Calvin had to accept the blame for any blunders. He knew there was no room for bargaining with the powers that be.

The message was crystal clear to Calvin. The children must be swiftly silenced to enable the completion of his assignment. There was no time for them to simply fall under control as easily as the complex management employees had.

Calvin pushed in the key, and his car trunk yawned widely. He could hear the sound of angry rasping metal as thousands of ants raged against one another in the sealed two-gallon glass jars. He unscrewed the lids and dropped small scraps of Sarah's and Billy's homework inside of each jar. The ants converged on the paper and burned it to ash. But in unison, the ants now knew the scent of their primary victims. Each jar was alive with thousands of squirming, thrashing ants that were impatiently awaiting the opportunity to attack their two new targets.

Calvin became immersed in the sensation of escalating pressure inside his head. His brain began thrusting to expand in every direction. The pulsing rhythm increased to a deafening pitch. The jars began to vibrate as the ants rallied and responded to Calvin's brain waves, which broadcast the message to the ants from their Queen. Calvin staggered under the intense pain. He could feel an unstoppable surge of bile rising from his stomach and stumbled toward the bushes to release the bitter fluid.

Calvin drove back to the complex with his entrusted cargo secure in the trunk of the Volvo. His head was throbbing, and his body was still weak and shaking. He cut the engine, turned the car lights out, and silently rolled into the parking lot near buildings "A" and "B".

The evening had begun. It was nightfall, and the residents were home and tucked inside the safe haven of their cozy apartments. The Queen was anxious to take charge of her new domain. Each building was a fortress. Calvin's job was to penetrate them one by one and secure them under the command of the Queen.

Calvin had arrived in time to observe the four of them hurrying down the sidewalk from Billy's building towards Sarah's. Calvin realized that it would certainly save time and simplify things since the two children were together. Sarah's building was the first on the list to be conquered. The whole complex would be under the Queen's control by the end of the evening.

Tomorrow was the prime shopping day. Ants would be deposited in supermarkets and forge their way into the homes of the Town residents. On Sunday, Calvin would disperse the ants at the churches where they could tag a ride back to the homes of the worshippers. By Monday, at the end of the last lunch period, the school students and teachers would be hers. She would have control of all their families by Monday evening. There would be no stopping the Queen's grand plan as it silently spread until the Town was thoroughly infiltrated and had become her center of command.

The Hunt Begins

Chapter 16

They arrived at Sarah's apartment just as Matt's phone rang. It was Julie. She relayed to Matt her flight had been canceled. Matt agreed to look after Sarah for the night.

Billy walked slowly into each room with Mouse on his shoulder while they tapped on the target areas to agitate any ants that might be concealed. Matt aimed the heat detector gun over the walls, ceilings, floors, and furniture. They checked each drawer and closet, working their way back towards Sarah's bedroom. Mouse remained silent but watchful.

Maggie was taken aback when Sarah opened the door to her room. One whole wall was framed and covered in corkboard, and the artwork on display was stunning.

"Yeah," said Sarah, "I love it. Mom and I just refinished the wall. At least this way, there are not a million holes because of me hanging my work. I like to lie in bed and study the unfinished pieces. We got permission to do it, as long as we paid for it. It went up pretty easy, but we had to use quite a bit of adhesive spray." Sarah showed Maggie the remaining two spray cans.

"Billy used to have a huge blackboard on his wall. When he was in second grade, he was trying to figure out how to harness lightning into usable electricity. We made the blackboard for him because we couldn't find one large enough for his continuous illustrations." Maggie gave Billy a smile.

"I think I am pretty close to the answer now," Billy said. "Hey, those ideas are still on my back burner."

Mouse started to chatter when they neared the art table. The heat detector registered a cluster of warmth in Sarah's box of art brushes. At the bottom of the box, sure enough, they found a cluster of ants. The ants immediately started to scatter, but Matt secured them to Sam's magnet with one pass over the box.

"Well, that worked sweetly," Matt said to Billy. "I'm counting fifteen of them."

Mouse had settled down on Billy's shoulder and watched intently. Matt double-checked the ceilings and walls in case any clusters of ants might be hidden behind the drywall or wood trim. After searching the entire apartment, no further ants were found.

The next apartment to be checked was Maggie's. It would be pretty late by the time they checked through every room, so they all agreed to stay together overnight. At least they would feel safer and know everyone was OK.

Desperate Measures

Chapter 17

Sarah grabbed a change of clothes and headed for the bathroom to pack a few necessary items for the overnight.

Mouse noticed it first. He began squealing and bouncing wildly on Billy's shoulder. An eight-inch wide swath of ants had gained access into the apartment. They entered from under the apartment door and were swiftly moving across the kitchen floor.

Matt handed his cell phone to Maggie. "Call the Fire Department! Tell them that we need them fast. Tell them that we found something combustible in the apartment and give the address."

Matt bolted to the door and swung it open. Caught by surprise, Calvin Phelps was kneeling on the hall floor, pouring the ants under the door. Matt grabbed the glass jar and slid it into the apartment. He brought his fist up sharply under Calvin's chin and knocked him unconscious. Matt capped the jar swiftly and halted the release of literally thousands of ants that still remained in the container. A second empty container lay in the hall.

He turned just in time to see Billy run towards the bathroom. Sarah had let out a piercing wail for help. The ants were streaming under the door and into the bathroom.

Mouse jumped off Billy's shoulder and onto the bathroom floor. His teeth were chattering, and his tail was lashing as he faced off some of the ants. Just as the ants were preparing to circle Mouse and close in, he made his escape by leaping upon the vanity. The confusion the mouse created stalled the progress of the ants that had targeted Sarah. Mouse continued to chatter. The mouse ran like mad back and forth on the vanity top.

In desperation, Billy yelled to his mother, "Mom, quick, get the two cans of adhesive from Sarah's room. There are too many ants for the magnet to handle."

Sarah was standing on the inside rim of the tub. The ants had mounded into a pyramid, using their bodies to overcome the slippery side of the tub. Once they were able to pyramid to the top of the outside wall of the tub, they tumbled into the tub. They had now begun building another pyramid formation on the back wall of the tub in order to get to Sarah. It was evident that Sarah was the target the ants were homing in on. The ants were agitated enough that Billy could see they were glowing red hot even with the bathroom light turned on.

Maggie ran to the door of the bathroom and threw the two cans of spray to Billy. He tossed Sarah one of the cans. "Spray your heart out!" He told her.

They both began locking the ants in place with the spray adhesive. Billy kept a wet line of spray on the floor at the doorway so no more ants could enter. The ants that were now turned away at the doorway began a confused clustering and circling on the ceramic kitchen floor.

Billy called out from the bathroom, "It's working. They are getting stuck, but these cans are running out of spray. They're angry, and they're hotter than the fourth of July."

Matt dashed Maggie out the apartment door and gave her his truck keys. "Get me the gallon of floor adhesive in the back of my truck. It's got a blue lid, and grab the pack of paintbrushes. I need it fast, really fast." Matt kept watching with the magnet by the bathroom door. It was already nearly loaded with squirming ants.

Calvin Phelps began to stir. Matt ripped down several slat shades, thinking he would use the cord to tie up Calvin and hold him for the police. As he moved forward to take action, the Firemen arrived, and they filled the doorway. They were astounded at the situation.

Matt directed them quickly, "Get everyone out of the building fast. These things are not what they look like. They can ignite a fire within seconds." The situation looked strange at best, but Matt was one of their co-workers, and they knew and trusted his judgment. The firefighters immediately set about evacuating the building. Once the doorway area was clear again, Matt's heart sunk as he saw that Calvin had taken the opportunity to slip away unnoticed.

Maggie came running breathlessly into the apartment. "Matt, I found it all."

Matt ripped open the bucket before running to the entrance of the bathroom. The ants had been either stuck in the adhesive or held at bay at the door. The spray was nearly dry, and ants were clustered and waiting to cross the drying barrier. He painted a new line across the doorway with the paintable floor adhesive.

Billy helped Sarah down from the tub ledge, then took the mouse off the vanity and gave him to Sarah. "Put him in your sweatshirt pocket before he gets tangled up with the ants."

Billy jumped over the line at the doorway. He grabbed one of Matt's brushes and painted a thick line of adhesive on the kitchen floor, and stood in front of it. "Watch, it's Sarah and me that they are after." His point was proven when the ants began flocking toward Billy.

Matt continued making the design into an L shape. "Let's corral them into this area and seal up all four sides."

Maggie grabbed the metal magnet and tried to gather up any stray ants beyond the sticky lines. The magnet was already overloaded with writhing ants and only had enough open surface area for a few more.

Billy motioned Sarah out of the bathroom. "Come on. Let's dance!" They both jumped inside and outside the lines to lure the opposition until all the ants were stuck in goo or within the boundary of the large area of adhesive drawn on the floor.

Matt painted the fourth line on the floor and sealed the ants within a square of goo. The ants were seething red hot by this time, but there was no danger of them igniting anything on the ceramic surface. Matt dropped gobs of floor adhesive on the majority of sequestered ants. The entrapped ants were pulsing red hot, and the square on the floor was flashing like a neon sign. One of the firefighters returned and sprayed the square and the bathroom floor with a fire extinguisher.

The police arrived to assist with the evacuation. They agreed that all five buildings needed to be checked and the school. Maggie informed the police that the science teacher had been found pouring the ants into Julie's apartment. The police searched the premises. Calvin was not in his apartment, and his car was nowhere to be found in the parking lot. A call went out to search for and stop the rented Volvo with the license number that Sarah gave the officers.

Exhaustion Rules

Chapter 18

It was nearly midnight before they headed over to Matt's house, which was a safe twenty minutes away, and out of the confusion the evacuation caused. They all tapped their cell phones just to be on the safe side before they entered his house.

Matt shook his head. "I don't think I'll mention this to the Fire Department, but they just laid out forty thousand dollars for a heat sensor when a mouse can do the same job."

They sat down to bowls of soup and crackers, then settled in for the camp out on Matt's living room floor with quilts, sleeping bags, and pillows. They all needed the sense of security that being safely huddled together in the same room gave them.

Matt smiled in relief now that it all was behind them. "So this is what Friday night with a family is all about. This family stuff is pretty exhausting if you ask me. It's hard to believe what we just went through and everything that went on. Crazy stuff, but the problem started in Sarah's box of art supplies, and what we needed to solve our troubles was one of her art supplies. We had to think fast, but we got darn lucky figuring out what to do to stop them."

Maggie was totally done in. "I think we make an exceptional team. I have to admit I will never complain about a plain old Friday night again."

"I'll even settle for a movie I've seen ten times before and fries, of course." Billy laughed and shook his head.

Sarah pulled her quilt up around her. "Where do you think the ants came from?"

"Who knows? Maybe we'll never know," Maggie answered. "Out of nowhere, just like the mouse. I don't even want to start wondering about it tonight. By the way, Mr. Science, did you give the police all the other ants we collected?"

"I can truthfully say, I turned over all the ants I had." Billy glanced over at Sarah, but she seemed to be asleep, or at least she looked like she was. Sarah still had her ant safely encased in adhesive. She had sworn Billy into secrecy because, at some point, they both wanted to dismantle it under the microscope. It was so strange that the facts were not likely to be disclosed in the newspaper. Even if it were possible for them to cut it apart, they would never find out the whole truth about it.

Sarah had confided to Billy that she heard her mother tell someone on the phone that Uncle Matt was really, really, really interested in his mom. All Billy thought of as he drifted off was how good it was to feel like a whole family again.

Mouse curled up in Billy's slipper. No one made any move to turn the lamp lights out, and one by one, they drifted off into well-deserved sleep.

Departure Comes Swiftly

Chapter 19

Calvin drove up the winding road to the high ridge. He had put the Town thirty miles behind him. There would be a steep price to pay for his failure. Right at the moment, he relished the silence in his head. His current lack of pain only meant the Queen was deliberating his fate.

He had to agree the mission had undoubtedly come to a futile end, but in his defense, he had followed all her orders precisely as they were given to him. The two children had managed to foul up the carefully laid plans. Children are frequently unpredictable. He had learned that years ago when he was an ordinary science teacher.

With all the confusion at the apartment complex, Calvin knew he had driven beyond where they would start looking for him. He slowed his speed and rolled down his window to enjoy the night air. At least, he would be leaving before the military got involved. The two children hardly knew anything, only that they found strange ants. He had no choice, but to leave thousands of nonfunctional ants behind, which was enough to foster an endless government study. It would be far worse if he ended up in government hands. They had their ways of extracting the truth.

The last message he had received from the livid Queen ant still echoed in his brain. "You botched the job, Calvin Phelps. Return immediately and report to the experimental lab for slave humans. As insects, all we can do for now is to continue to plague your species until we develop a more fail-safe plan. We are billions, and humans already seek to control their population. Our time will come. All humans will eventually become our slaves and do our bidding. We will not settle for the crumbs of the earth."

Calvin reached the top of the ridge. He saw the ship was already there waiting. He got out of the car and dropped his rental car keys on the seat. For a moment, he ran his hand over the edge of the Corinthian leather seat and locked the sensation of its smoothness into his memory. He took a few deep breaths of fresh, clean air and thought about how enjoyable it had felt to drive a car again. He looked down at the peaceful valley below where the countryside was dotted with distantly lit homes and street lights. His fondest memories of earth were always centered around the little, simple, pleasant things in life and certainly not his numerous, massive blunders.

There was no turning back. The punishment for even thinking about escaping was too painful to survive. There was no way to free himself of the implant in his head that forced him to do their bidding. The Queen Ant had her own agenda. She seemed to forget her kind was created by a human. The man with the brown triangle in his eye was still being forced to keep improving her kind. Calvin hoped that man would be the one to dole out his punishment. The man was a human being too, and Calvin could hope that the man still harbored a shred of compassion within him.

Calvin walked briskly to the ship and boarded, only turning around once to take a last glance at the planet that had once been his home.

The ship lifted off silently, began to rotate, and disappeared into the starlit sky with a flash.

The Final Chapter

Chapter 20

Mouse stirred and climbed up on Billy's shoulder. He thumped his foot several times. Billy was so exhausted he didn't even stir. He glanced over at Sarah, and he could tell by her light, even breathing, that she too was asleep. Maggie and Matt were deep in the throes of well-deserved rest.

Mouse scampered over to the dining room window and gazed up at the sky. The full moon lit up the yard with a soft glow. All looked peaceful and quiet. It was time.

He bit into the base of his tail and removed a tiny communicator. He carefully keyed in the awaited message. "The 'Mission Ant-imation' has been successfully aborted. Invader ants have all been secured. If we keep our own kind's population in balance, we can cohabitate easily and peacefully with the humans."

The response came swiftly, "Excellent work, Number 605998. Destroy your communicator and proceed to enjoy your new life on earth." Mouse climbed down from the windowsill and deposited his tiny communicator in the kitchen trash can. He took some of Sarah's burn cream off the kitchen counter and rubbed it over the new cut in his tail. It would heal in a day or two. He stretched and then curled back up in Billy's slipper.

Earth was a marvelous place where his kind could blend right in. Given the earth's atmosphere, he could at least hope his species could stay small in size and, therefore, go unnoticed. But to keep things on the safe side, he made up his mind that it was probably best to control his intake of calories.

His mission had been a complete success. He had helped stop the alien ant invasion, and it was time to enjoy his reward. He wasn't just a number anymore. He belonged now. He was part of a family, and he had his own very special name. His name was Mouse.

About the Author

Although a native of Western New York for most of her life, the author of this book also resided for ten years in a cabin, deep in the bowels of Appalachian coal-mining country, close to nature, on the edge of Braddock's Run and the wilderness of Savage Mountain. It was a well-learned lesson concerning how formidable wildlife, nature, and individuals can be. The author never came face to face with a cougar in the mountains, but after her return to the Buffalo, NY area, she did have one wander into her naturalized backyard. The author began writing fiction when no one chose to believe her stories concerning actual events. So it goes.

The author gardens profusely, wintering many plants in her home with an attached greenhouse. She finds that the writing of fiction is similar to gardening. Some characters planted in a novel are allowed to flourish, some fill in the necessary groundwork, and some are fated to die on the vine. Sometimes nurturing a character requires intense hoeing.

The author's fictional writing interests range from adventure in the ancient past, current times, or a future world. Following the lead of whatever inspires her, the author adheres to the principle that the reader deserves a good ride. The author's unfinished stories reside in a folder entitled "Spits in the Wind."